THE PRIEST: THE FILTY MAN IN WHITE

I AM A PRIEST ALTHOUGH I NEVER WANTED TO BE ONE

LUCY FESTUS

ONE

I woke up soaked in sweat. oh it was all a dream! damn she was beautiful. There comes the annoying knock on the door from my servant boy "good morning, Father "comes the unpleasant voice, good morning, Sam I answered. I stood up and washed myself with the thoughts of her firm breasts on my mind oh! I have never seen any like it and her full lips bless me. I felt my dick harden, I could have helped myself with my lotion but I had to lead the morning mass. Sam knocked again oh that boy does everything to remind me of my priesthood "Father, Father" he called disrupting my line of thought "what do you need" It's almost time for mass he answered, okay Sam, I replied.

Wondering who I am? My name is Tom Smith and I am the last of seven children. My parents John and Kate Smith are devoted Catholics, my sisters Rose, Lucy, Grace, Tina, Sophia, Bianca and Faith are all married to different men with children. Most importantly I am priest who doesn't want to be one. Father! your breakfast is served, Sam called again. I stepped out of my room to the table, had breakfast and rushed off to church. With my perfectly rehearsed smile I lead the morning mass, blessed the children and closed the service. I sat in my office to go through some paper work I needed to fill out then the memory of the last confession of a member came to mind. "Forgive me father for I have sinned" were his words, take your confession I replied. I fucked a girl last night and she is not my wife he said, I felt my penis move in my trousers. She seduced me he continued, I promised my wife that I would never cheat on her but I couldn't help it Father, he said. I urged him to continue and he went on "she stripped herself naked in my office and inserted her fingers in her vagina, she fucked herself and moaned until I could no longer hold back. My manhood pushed itself out and I didn't know when I kissed her and began to do everything, she ordered me to do. I fucked her very wet pussy and sucked her boobs until I came crashing into her, she was so warm and soft. I could not look at her after the deed was done, Father. I advised him to stay faithful and stay away from sin, gave him his penance and he left. Now

I'm stuck with the thoughts of him fucking a random girl in his office I guess this is the only part of being a priest I enjoyed. The day went by swiftly and I hurried back to my room for some privacy which I needed. I slept off the minute my head touched my pillow and there she was in my sleep with the firmest breasts and fullest lips I have ever seen "Come to me" she called and I ran like a scared child into her arms.

She held me tight and kissed me deeply like her life depended on it, her soft lips held on to mine and her hands were in my trousers caressing my already hard dick. Then she whispered into my ears do you want me to use my mouth on it" she pointed to my shorts and I screamed yes excitedly, she instructed me to lie on my back which I did like an obedient student and she looked into my eyes and said "you would enjoy this' and buried her face in between my legs. First it felt warm and then I lost my senses, I felt her lips grip my penis and sucked softly like a newborn on breasts. She used her tongue to circle the base of my manhood and used her fingers on my asshole then she started sucking the tip I could feel myself cumming but she stopped and looked at me with dim eyes, she separated my legs and mounted me, oh I felt her dripping pussy on my cock and she started to ride me like a horse and she called out my name Tom! do you really want to continue being a priest? No! "Fuck me" I muttered, "I am" she responded, "hard" I commanded and she put my hands to her breast and rode me until I felt my sperm pouring and I let out a loud moan. I held on to her, smelling her hair and body then I remembered I don't know her before I could ask what her name is, I heard a knock that woke me from my sleep. Father! Sam called yes, I responded, your dinner is served. I tried to stand but felt weak and I realized my shorts were soaked with sperm and smiled. I rushed to the bathroom, had a warm bath and went to the dinning room for dinner. Dinner was boring as usual I always wished I had a wife and children to eat with but no is just Sam, in his shorts exposing his penis size which I have noticed is on the big side for a boy his age. We ate quietly with him smiling shyly at me I wondered what he was thinking throughout the meal. I left to my room and slept like a log although I wished for her to show up but she did not.

TWO

Good morning! I heard above me as I gently opened my eyes, I saw Sam looking down at me stack naked. He smiled softly and for the first time in three years I notice is perfect set of white teeth, well I put myself together and asked why he was naked in my room and he said "I have seen the way you look at my penis father and I was hoping you could touch it" I faked a frown and asked him to leave but he kissed me instead I tried to push him away then I realized that I enjoyed the kiss. Sam turned his butt hole to me as he played with my penis, I looked down at him and saw how handsome he was, he let out a moan when I penetrated him and his hole was so tight that I came immediately but he didn't stop. He knelt down and sucked my dick until it got hard again, I fucked him over and over again I didn't want to stop but the church bell brought me back to priesthood and I as came for the fifth time Sam said the words, I dread the most "I love you Father". I saw the disappointment in his eyes when I said nothing. Breakfast was awkward because Sam didn't look up at me or smile shyly like he use to but I didn't let it bother me as I figured it was related to what had happened in the early hours of the day. left for my office and served communion later that evening.

I arrived at my house and met Sam's absence though I thought he left instead the gateman told me he went out to get foodstuffs. I quickly entered my room and locked the door behind me in order to avoid Sam but I could not stop myself from reflecting on what happened that morning and then came the knock followed by his voice dinner is served father he mumbled. I went to the table and ate hurriedly without looking up, I could feel his eyes on me. I took a long shower and prepared for bed when I heard a tap on my door, I ignored at first but then it came again, come in Sam I said and there he was naked again. What do you want? I asked, pretending not to know what he was after. "I want you to repeat what you did to me in the morning" he whispered bending towards me and grabbing me. I kissed him and played with his asshole softly then I penetrated him with my huge cock I heard him call the holy name as I fucked him hungrily like a caveman, he came same time as me. He tried to leave but I asked him not to and we slept holding each other close. I woke up in the middle of the night to see Sam sleeping curled beside me. I was amazed by his beauty his blond hair and full pink lips were so beautiful that I was forced to ask myself if I have been blind these past years.

THREE

I woke up cold and didn't feel Sam beside me, my curtains were drawn. He had gone to clean up and prepare breakfast I believed. Even so, I stepped out of bed and entered the bathroom to get set for the day.

At shortly after two p.m., I drove to my family home and my father travelled by wheelchair to my car. He insisted on wheeling himself despite my insistence that I propel him prudently, as a good son should.

I sat beside my mother in our old living room while she kept on blabbing about how proud she was to have me as her son. The lord has favored me she said beaming with smiles, I listened as she went on and on about how she was the envy of all the women in the church because I was a priest. I left after a few hours to return to the parish and as I drove into my compound there he was smiling and singing happily like he had won a lottery. Sam, I called out to him, yes father. Meet me inside I said without looking up at him, Father you have a guest and she said her name is Ivon. I recognized her by her hair and dimple in her chin, since neither was easily altered. She wore a bright red dress and light make up. Ivon was my girlfriend before my mother forced priesthood on me, she strode straight to me and kissed me.

"Tom its wonderful to see you, you look worn-out".

"How's the church treating your bad ass

Your crazy sex libido. What are you thinking about?

"Our last night together and why you are here".

"Well, first the thing that went through my mind was me surviving without your huge cock. I couldn't possibly imagine my life without it".

"Do you want to see my room?" I asked

"Yes please, I hope you have a touch of red in there".

It started to rain heavily outside and I heard Sam close the main door, as I lead Ivon to my room. She sat on the bed and sniffed my sheets, thank God Sam changed them I thought to myself. She began to undress and asked for directions to my bathroom which I showed her with hesitation. I left her shortly to instruct Sam on what to prepare for dinner, I met him sobbing in the kitchen.

"What happened?" I queried

"You took her to your bedroom and I know you will do to her what you do to me".

So? I asked

"I'm jealous" he blurted out

Get a hold of yourself I am a priest and no one can have to themselves, "**I belong to everyone**" Sam, I continued, make rice for dinner please.

I could feel his eyes on me as I walked out of the kitchen but I didn't care about feelings I am a priest who doesn't want to be one after all. Ivon was nude when I walked into my bedroom, with her legs apart she beckoned on me to join her and I did.

I slowly inserted my fingers into her wet vagina, one then two, three and finally four. I found her g spot and hit it consecutively with my index finger, spanking and tapping it lovingly. She grabbed the sheets, shut her eyes and moaned like her life depended on it. At this point my penis was as hard as a rock and I spread her legs and slowly penetrated, slowly intensifying my speed. The more I slammed into her the wetter she became, I allowed my full length to project and prop for easier and faster thrusts, I felt her legs shaking and there came the squirt. Ivon began to scream as she came I groaned all of a sudden collapsing on her body. She kissed me passionately and whispered to me ," Father Tom run away with me". I stood up and went to have dinner with Sam because Ivon said she was not hungry. I left my house and went out of town to an exclusive club where nobody would recognize me leaving Ivon and Sam behind. I partied all night in the club with strangers, dancing and drinking alcohol until I felt a tap on my shoulder accompanied with a question "Are you father Tom"? asked the sweet young lady who was putting on almost nothing.

"Yes I am" and who are you?

"Reverend sister Mary" she replied

Guess I'm not the only rebel in the parish then. I spent the rest of the night in Mary's arms with too much alcohol in my system I can't give details of what transpired that night.

FOUR

In the early hours of Saturday morning I dressed up and left for my house while Mary was still sleeping completely nude in a room I can't remember how I got there. It was not easy to make Ivon understand why I could not run away with her like she wanted but I succeeded and she left disappointed. Sam was happy at her departure and didn't hide his excitement.

"Oh God I hope she never returns" he said

"Listen, I don't recommend falling in love with me I am priest and I belong to everyone".

Tom I have feeling and I have nursed my love for you over the years, I cannot kill them overnight he said in between tears as he ran off to his room.

Poor thing I said to myself and went to my room. At six p.m. I went to the chapel for a meeting and I saw sister Mary although she acted like nothing happened and smiled innocently at me I could tell she was up to no good. I rushed into my office to get off on some porn movie on my laptop then I head a knock on my door I quickly arranged myself and ordered the intruder in. Good day father Tom the young beautiful girl said, good day I replied with a SMIRK.

See you in the next part

www.ingramcontent.com/pod-product-compliance
Lightning Source LLC
Chambersburg PA
CBHW060933130726
48001CB00006B/2556